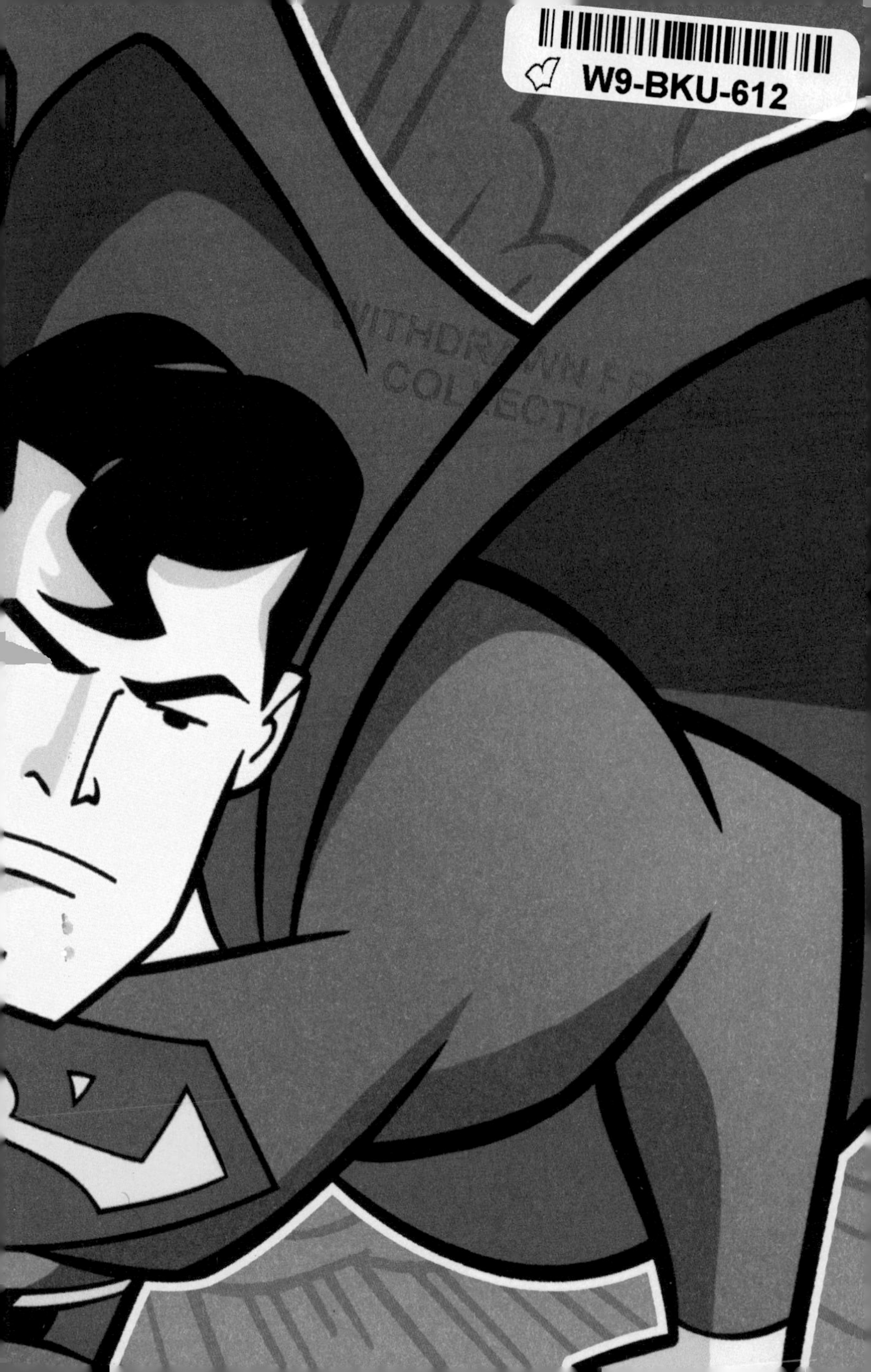

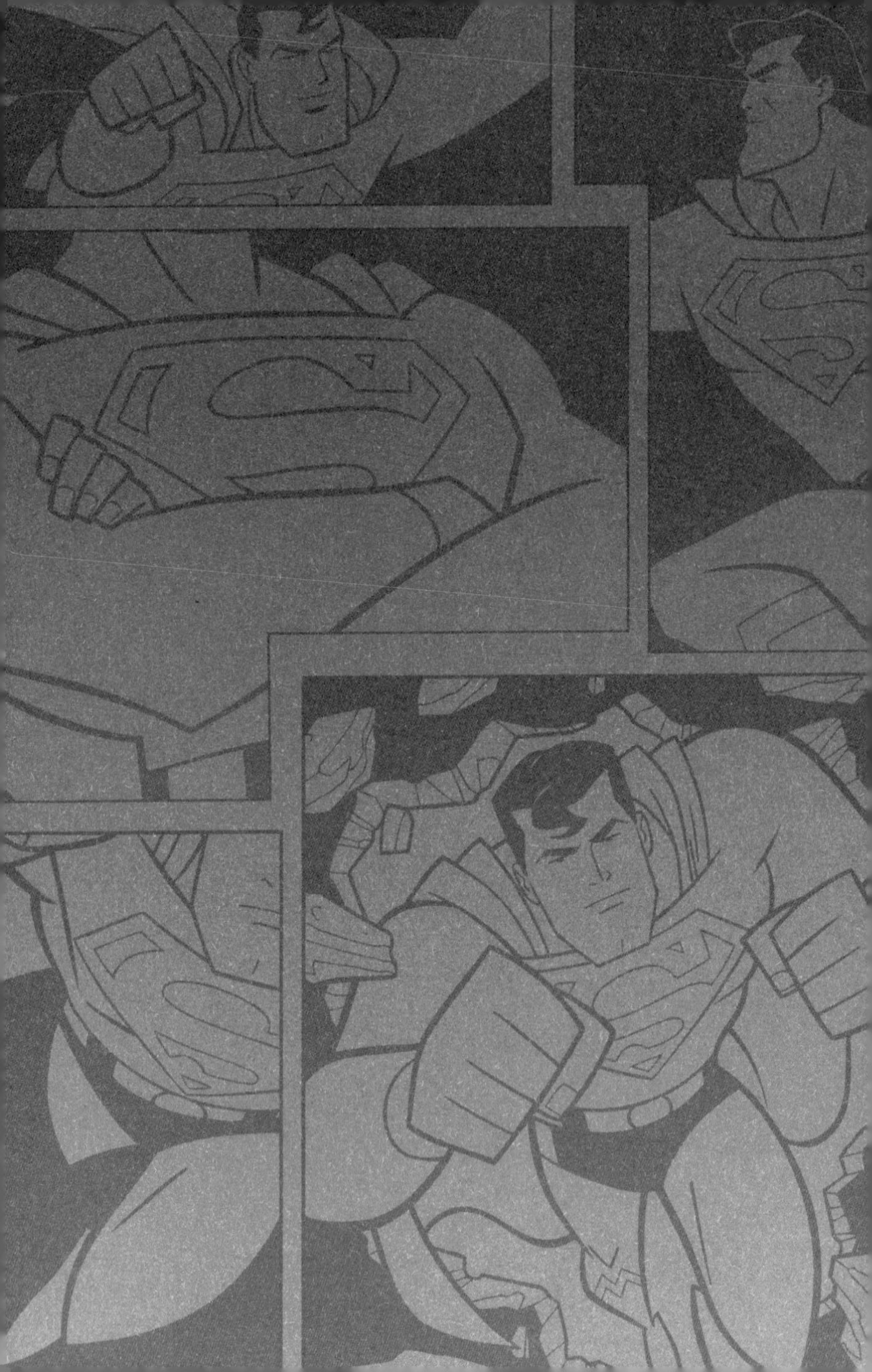

SUPERMAN

BIZARRO IS BORN!

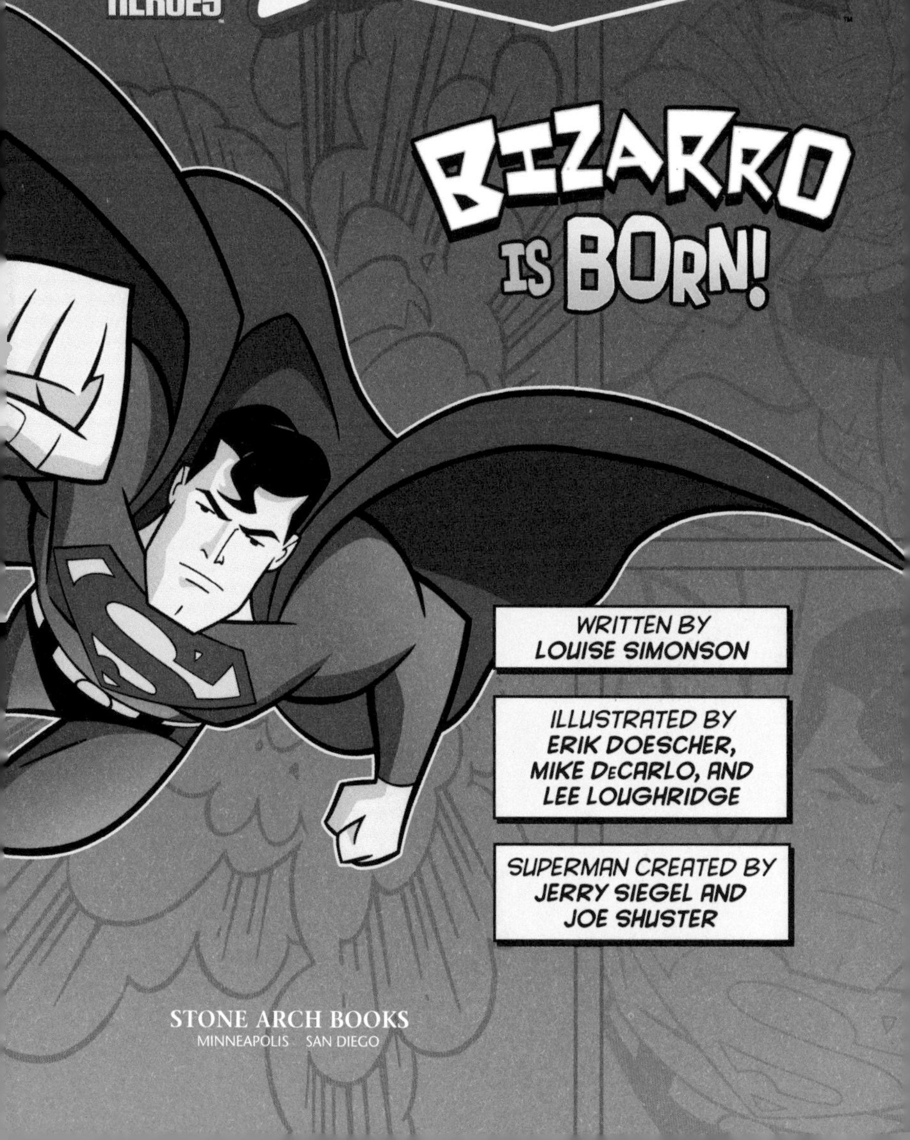

WRITTEN BY
LOUISE SIMONSON

ILLUSTRATED BY
ERIK DOESCHER,
MIKE DECARLO, AND
LEE LOUGHRIDGE

SUPERMAN CREATED BY
JERRY SIEGEL AND
JOE SHUSTER

STONE ARCH BOOKS
MINNEAPOLIS SAN DIEGO

Published by Stone Arch Books in 2010
151 Good Counsel Drive, P.O. Box 669
Mankato, Minnesota 56002
www.stonearchbooks.com

Library of Congress Cataloging-in-Publication Data

Simonson, Louise.
  Bizarro is born! / by Louise Simonson ; illustrated by Erik Doescher.
    p. cm. -- (DC super heroes. Superman)
  ISBN 978-1-4342-1567-3 (lib. bdg.) -- ISBN 978-1-4342-1725-7 (pbk.)
  [1. Superheroes--Fiction.] I. Doescher, Erik, ill. II. Title.
  PZ7.S605795Bi 2010
  [Fic]--dc22
                                        2009008737

Summary: *Daily Planet* reporter Lois Lane discovers that the evil Lex Luthor
has created his own tame Superman — Bizzaro Superman! Eventually, the
confused creature captures Lois and sets out on a path of destruction. The
real Superman must save Lois and stop Bizzaro before the monster destroys
Metropolis in a warped pursuit of truth, justice, and the American way.

Art Director: Bob Lentz
Designer: Bob Lentz

Printed in the United States of America

TABLE OF CONTENTS

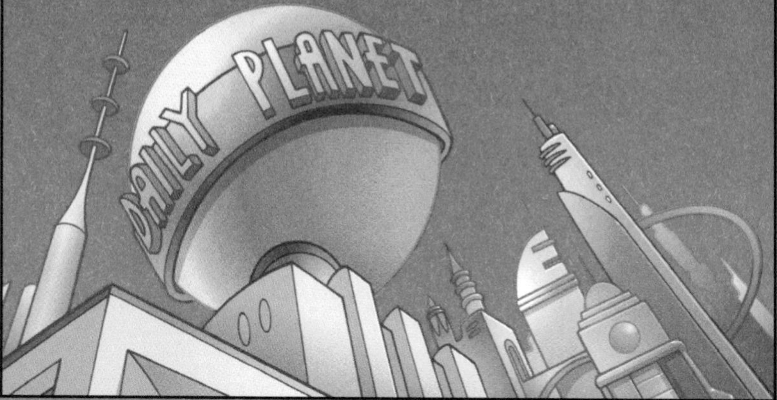

DAILY PLANET

CHAPTER 1

A REAL SUPER HERO

Superman hovered in the air, looking for danger. He smelled smoke. With his super-vision, he saw flames leap from the top floor of an old apartment building.

Sirens wailed as fire trucks rushed up the street. A woman ran down the sidewalk. "My children are inside!" she cried.

She tried to run into the building, but a policeman stopped her. Another officer stared up at the sky. "Look!" he shouted. "Superman is here!"

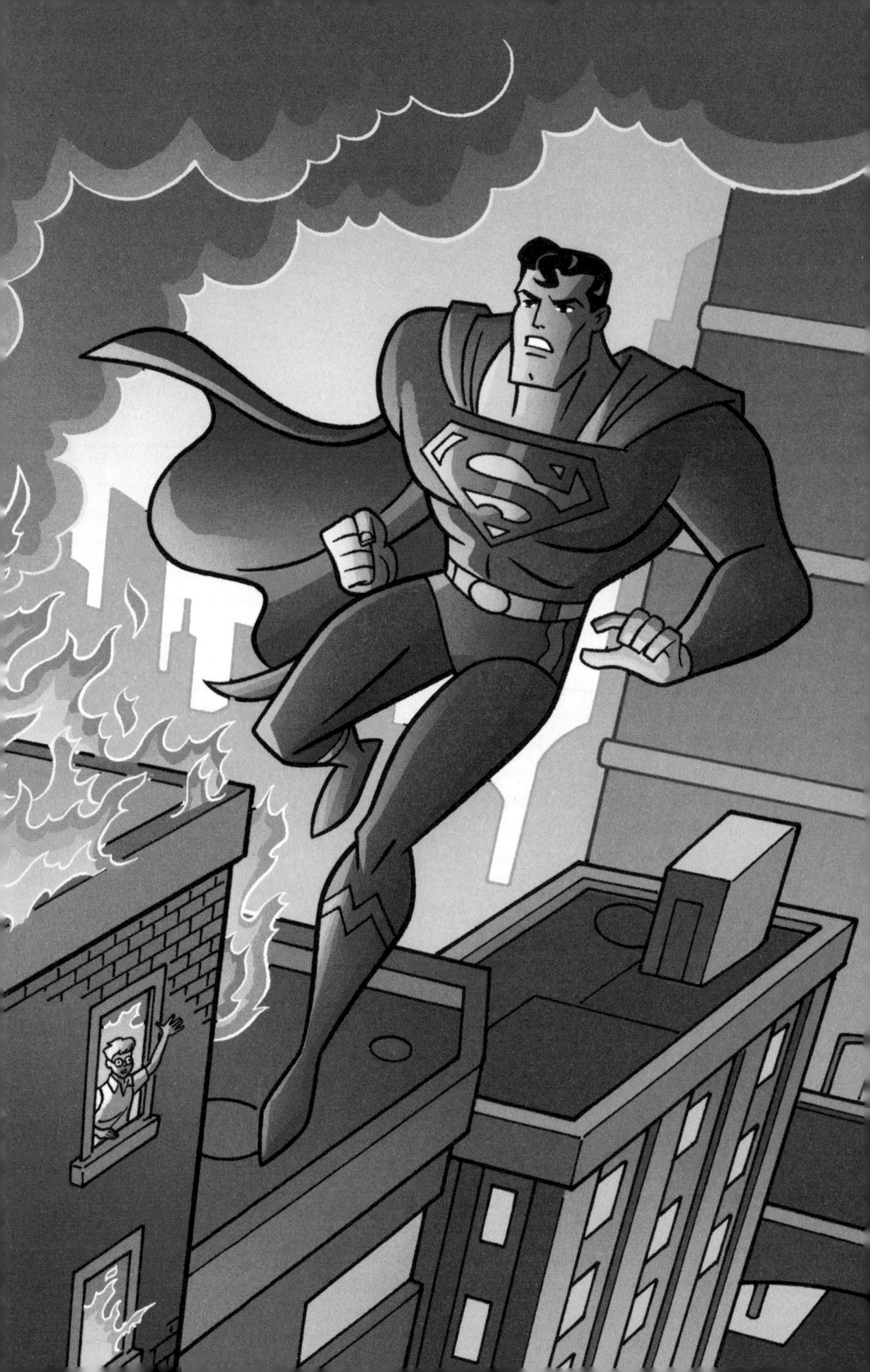

"Oh, thank goodness!" the woman said, sobbing. She knew her children would be safe now.

Superman was the world's greatest super hero. He was super-strong, faster than a speeding bullet, and had skin tougher than steel. Most importantly, Superman used his powers to help people.

Superman surveyed the building carefully with his X-ray vision. He saw that the two children were trapped in the bedroom by a wall of flames.

Superman flew to the bedroom window. The boy saw him and grinned.

"It's Superman!" the boy exclaimed.

Superman held out his hands, and the children climbed into his arms. Then, gently, he flew them away from danger.

Superman glided slowly to the ground. Then he placed the two children in the waiting arms of their mother.

"Thank you, Superman!" she said, grasping her children in her arms.

One of the firefighters ran over to the Man of Steel. "We sure could use your help," he said. "The fire won't go out!"

The super hero nodded. He flew directly above the burning building. He opened his mouth and blew out super-cold air.

WHOOOOSH! In less than a second, the air around the building froze. With no oxygen to fuel the flames, the fire quickly went out.

Everyone cheered. Superman smiled and waved to the people below.

I wish Lois were here, he thought.

Lois Lane was the *Daily Planet*'s star reporter. She always covered the stories about Superman, but she wasn't in the crowd today. Lois's boss, Perry White, had given her an assignment on a movie shoot, and Lois wasn't happy about it.

Superman was worried about Lois. He scanned the city using his super-vision and spotted her.

Lois and the young photographer, Jimmy Olsen, stood in the middle of a street beside a film crew. The street near the West River had been blocked off from traffic. A crowd of actors stood on the sidewalks waiting for filming to begin.

The movie director walked up the street to a couple of cars. He talked to the stunt drivers, then he pointed toward the camera. They were getting ready to film a car chase.

Lois looked grouchy. Beside her, Jimmy grinned as he took pictures.

"I'm glad you're having a good time," Lois grumbled.

"I thought you liked to be where the action is," Jimmy teased.

"I do," said Lois. "I just want the action to be real!"

Using his super-hearing, Superman could tell Lois was bored. He also knew her favorite jobs were often the ones that put her in danger. Superman was relieved to know that she would be safe on the set.

Superman soared above the city. He loved Metropolis. He looked down at the buildings where people lived and worked. He studied the rivers that ran beside the city and the low mountains beyond.

Factory buildings and high-tech research labs dotted their steep slopes. He even knew of a special government lab, called Project Cadmus, buried underground.

Superman landed on the roof of a tall building with a big, brass globe on top. This was the Daily Planet Building.

He opened the door to a small shed that led into a stairwell. He stepped inside and saw a business suit, neatly folded, where he had left it.

He changed into his suit at super-speed and put on his glasses. Then he raced down the steps.

ZWWWOOOOMMMM!

Disguised as Clark Kent, mild-mannered reporter, he opened the door to the newsroom.

Clark's boss, Perry White, stuck his head out of his office. "Clark, get in here!" he yelled.

Clark walked into Perry's office. "What's up, sir?" Clark asked.

"There was a fire in Hob's Bay," Perry began. "We'll need to —"

"I already covered the story," Clark interrupted. "I figured I would do it since Lois is on another assignment."

Perry sighed. "Oh right, the movie shoot," he said. "She wasn't happy about that assignment, but the readers will think it's interesting."

While Perry talked, Clark used his super-senses to check on Lois and Jimmy. They were still waiting beside the camera crew. The director was standing nearby.

"Lights, camera, and . . . action!" the director shouted.

SKKKREEEEEEE

A stunt car screeched down the street.

The second stunt car followed close behind. The driver swerved the first car toward the actors standing on the sidewalk. The actors ran and screamed. Then the car swerved back toward the camera. Jimmy was laughing, and Lois didn't look grumpy anymore.

Inside the Daily Planet newsroom, Clark smiled. The stunt drivers were good at their jobs. They made the car chase seem real and exciting. Clark turned his attention back toward Perry.

Then, suddenly, he heard Lois scream.

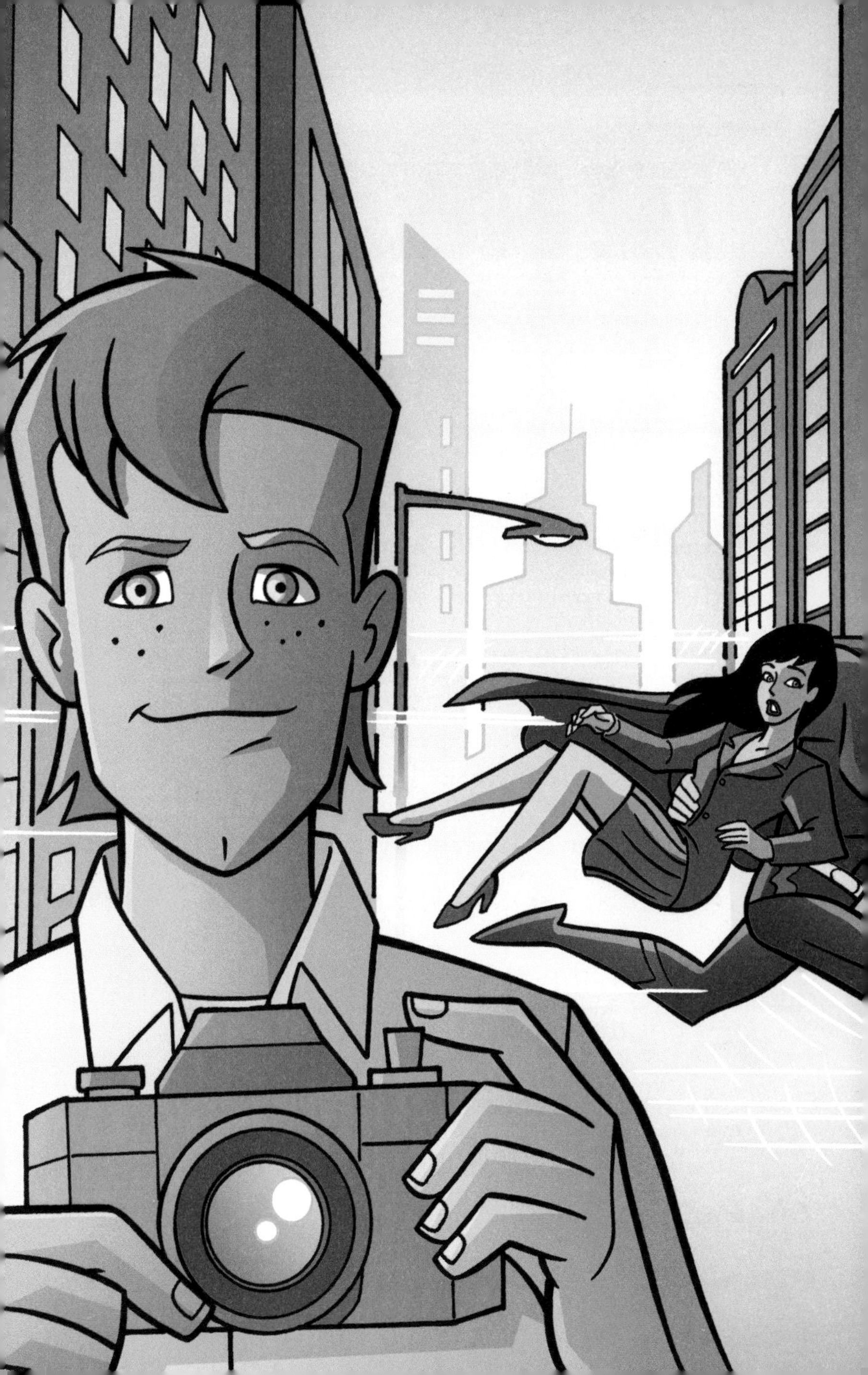

CHAPTER 2

THE SUPER-FAKE

Clark looked back toward the movie set with his super-vision. He saw the back of a flying man wearing a blue suit and red cape. The man was carrying Lois high into the air.

Clark frowned. The flying man was dressed just like Superman. Who was he?

Clark jumped to his feet. "I have to go, sir," he said. "Duty calls!"

He dashed through the newsroom doors and into the hall. He raced up the stairwell at super-speed, removing his suit as he ran.

Finally, wearing his blue and red Superman uniform, he dashed onto the roof and soared into the air.

• • •

Lois was feeling annoyed. One minute, she had been standing next to Jimmy, watching a camera crew film an exciting car chase. A second later, she felt herself being lifted into the air.

"You startled me," she muttered. "Superman, why did you do that?"

When Lois looked up at the man who was carrying her, she saw a blue costume and a red cape. Then she saw his skin was as white as chalk, and his forehead was large and stuck out strangely.

"Oh!" Lois shrieked. "You're not Superman! Who are you?"

"Me *am* Superman!" the white-faced man said. "Me save you from car. Lois, you my friend. Why you not know me?"

Lois stared at the white-faced man. He looked strong and scary, but his eyes were wide and innocent like a very young child's eyes.

He thinks he's Superman, Lois thought. *What's going on?*

Lois looked down. The film shoot was still going. Stunt cars swerved. Cameras filmed. All eyes were on the action.

"Those cars are in trouble!" the fake Superman said. "Them people need my help. Me show you me am Superman!"

Suddenly, the creature belched a cloud of red-hot fire from his mouth. **POOF!** The stunt cars burst into flames.

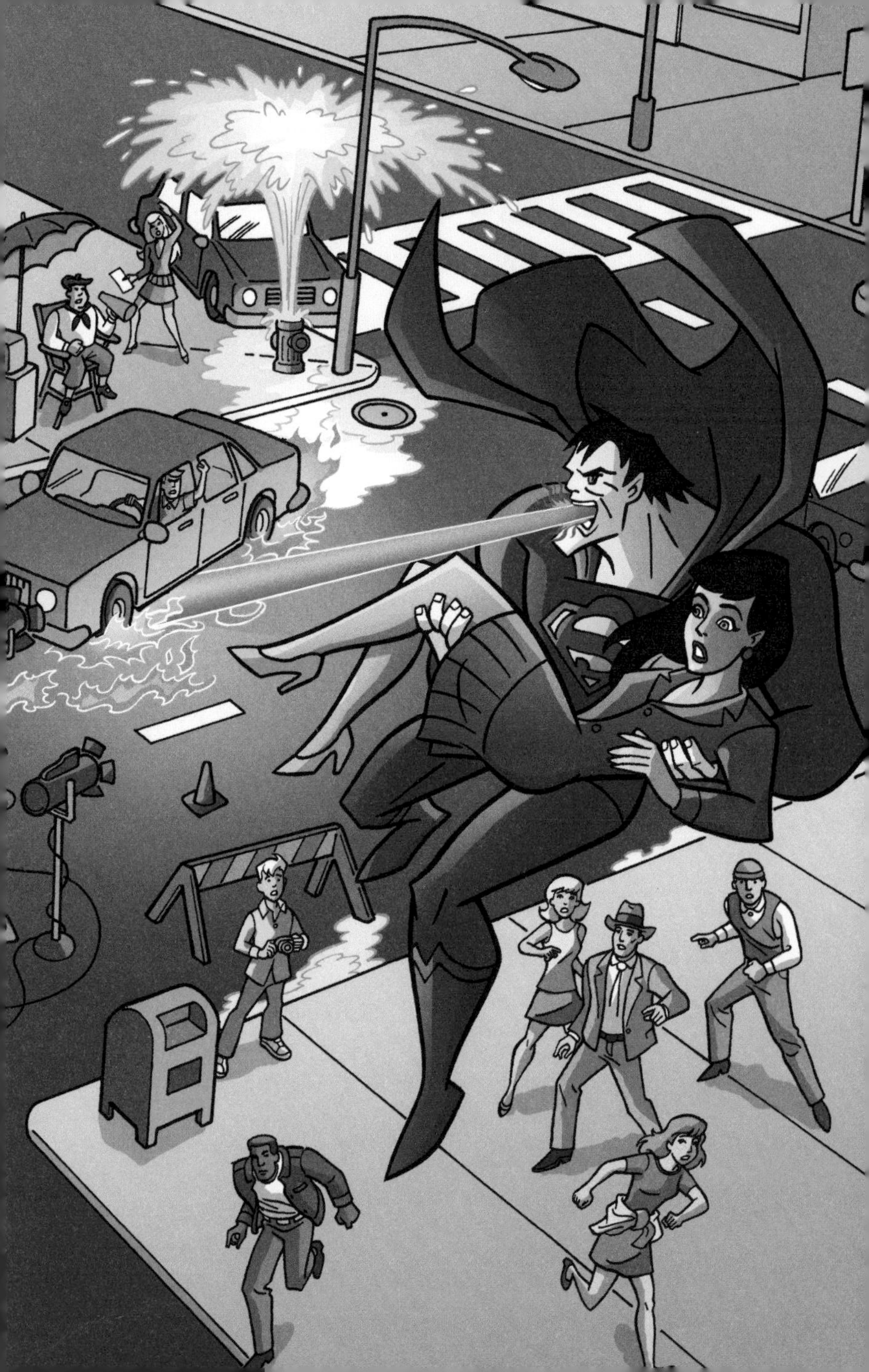

The first car swerved and slammed into a telephone pole.

The second car skidded and hit a fire hydrant. Water gushed high into the air.

"Why did you do that?" Lois asked.

"Me stop runaway cars," the fake Superman said proudly. "See? Cars not move anymore. Not hurt people. Me keep everybody safe!"

Meanwhile, the real Superman flew toward the movie set. He saw Lois, high up in the air, being held in the arms of the flying man wearing a costume just like his.

On the street below, two cars had crashed. One driver ran from his car. Half a second later, it burst into flames.

Then, with a loud **BOOM!** the other car burst into flames. That driver's door wouldn't open, and the man was stuck inside the burning vehicle.

Superman wanted to save Lois from the fake super hero, but he had to help the driver first. If the flames reached the gas tank, the car would explode. A lot of people would get hurt.

He landed beside the burning wreck and pulled off the door. Then he carefully lifted the stunt driver out of the car.

I need to smother the flames completely, Superman thought. *If a single spark is left, it could restart the fire.*

He lifted the flaming car into the sky. He carried it to the river, and dipped it gently into the water. **Hisssssss**

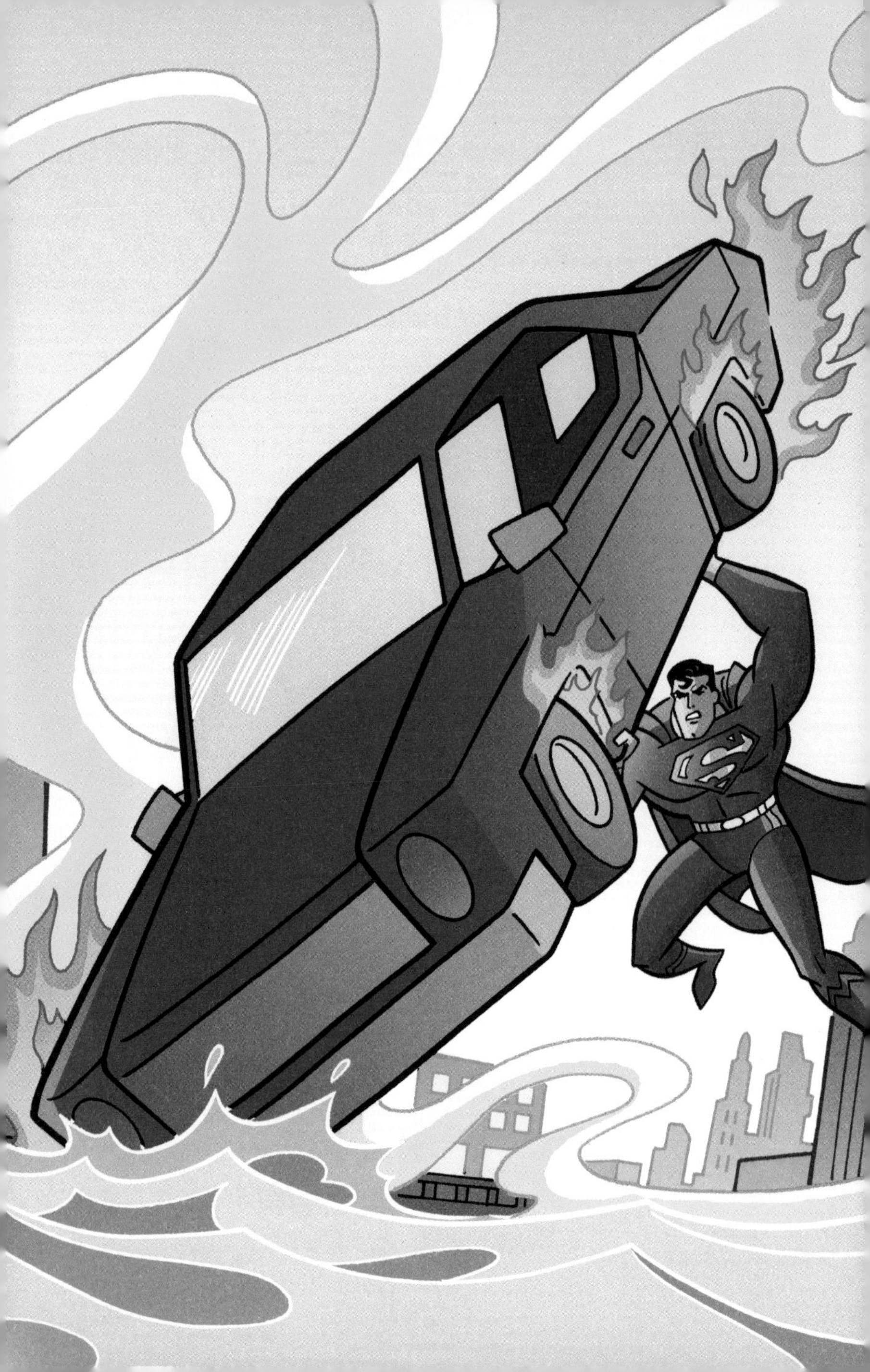

With the flames extinguished, Superman lowered the car back down to the ground.

As he hovered in the air, Superman used his super-vision to search for Lois and her kidnapper. He couldn't see them anywhere. Then, suddenly, he heard a familiar voice.

"Superman!" Jimmy shouted. "Some creep in a Superman outfit carried Lois toward the mountains!"

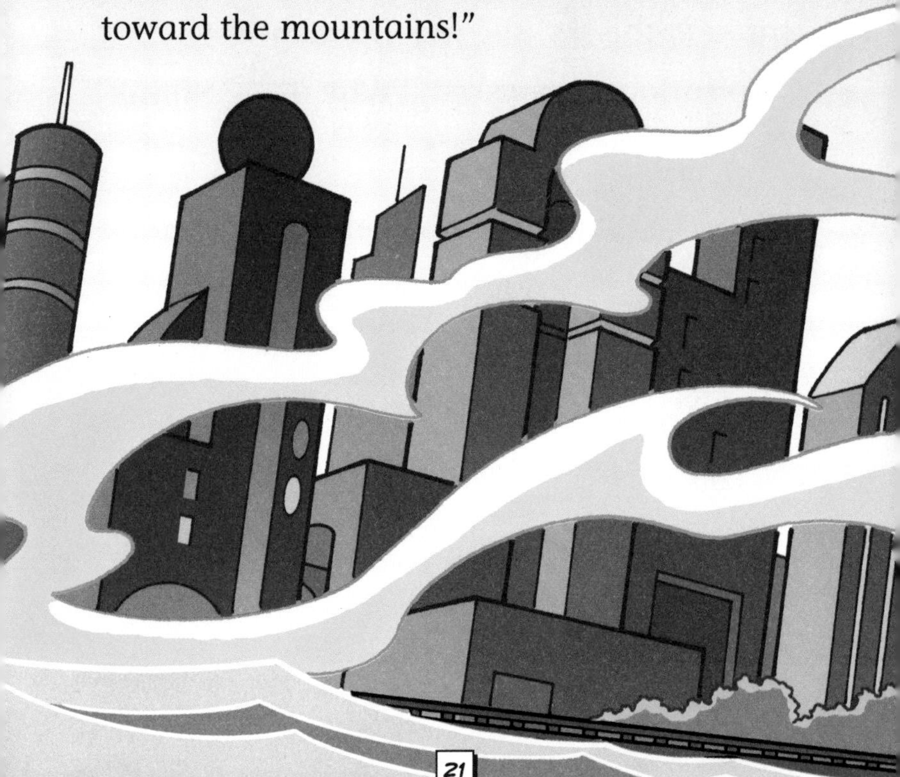

CHAPTER 3

THE BIZARRO PROJECT

As the fake Superman carried Lois through the sky, she was frightened, but also curious. She asked, "Why do you think you're Superman?"

"Me *am* Superman!" the fake Superman replied. "Me fly. Me shoot beams from eyes. Me super-strong. Me have skin like steel. Me save Lois. Me help people!"

Lois was being carried high into the sky. It seemed like a really bad time to argue with him. Instead, she asked, "Where do you live?"

The creature pointed west, toward the mountains that overlooked Metropolis. "Me live there," he said. "My home is called Secret Lab. Me sleep there and me practice being Superman."

Lois frowned. Someone had secretly created another Superman!

"Why did you stop the cars?" Lois asked.

"Me wake up and hear people yell for help," the creature said. "Dr. Teng not there. Nobody there. So me crash through wall. Then me see people run from cars. So me break cars. Me save you, too. You my friend, Lois Lane!"

He sounded so proud of himself that Lois couldn't resist smiling, but her mind was racing. This was big news. She wanted to cover the story, but she needed details.

"I'd like to see where you live. Can I see your Secret Lab?" Lois asked.

"Me take you there!" the super-fake said.

He carried Lois toward a windowless concrete building. As they came closer, Lois saw that one of the walls had a big hole in it. An alarm rang loudly.

"Is Dr. Teng inside the building?" she asked.

The fake Superman squinted. "Me can see through many things," he replied, "but me can't see through that wall."

"The building must be lined with lead," Lois told him. "It is the one thing Superman can't see through."

Lois wasn't surprised. Dr. Teng would have wanted to keep the lab a secret from everyone — especially Superman.

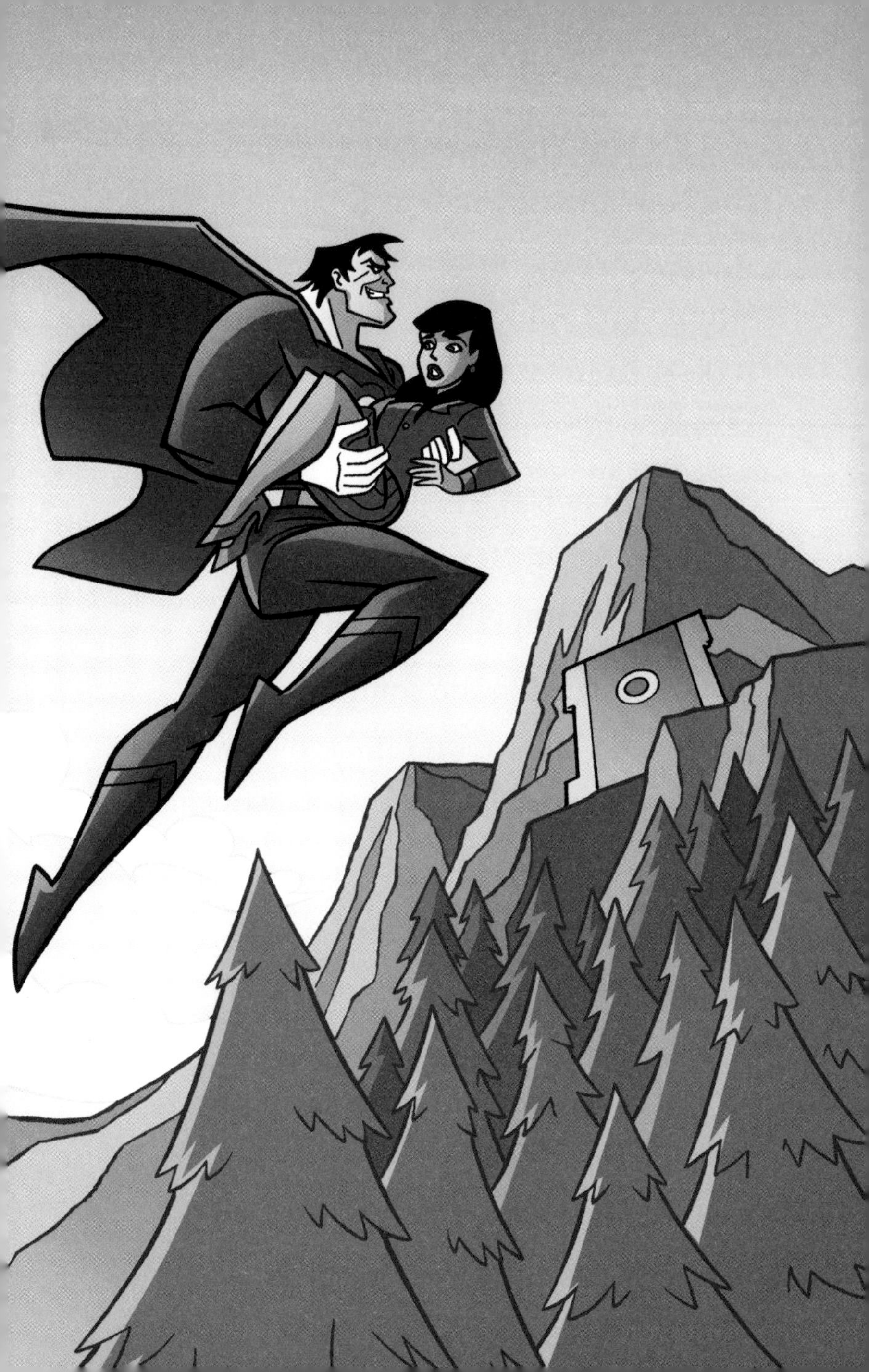

Lois and the super-fake flew through the hole into the high-tech lab. Lois looked around. The room was lined with science equipment. A big, heavy computer sat on a desk. In the center was a metal box with several wires running from it.

"That my bed," the creature said proudly. "Dr. Teng put wires in my head. Then me dream of being Superman."

Lois hurried to the computer and punched a button, and the screen lit up. There was one folder showing. It read: BIZARRO PROJECT.

Lois read the file quickly. It said that Dr. Teng had used Superman's DNA to make a super-clone. Teng had used wires to feed images of Superman's adventures into the clone's brain. He wanted the clone to think he was Superman.

The experiment hadn't worked. Teng's clone, Bizarro, had many problems, but the doctor wasn't ready to give up.

"This lab has lots of expensive equipment," Lois said. "I wonder where the money came from."

Quickly, she looked through the other files. Then she saw one file labeled "L.L."

"L.L.," Lois said. "I'd bet my career that those initials stand for Lex Luthor."

Lex Luthor was one of the richest and most powerful people in all of Metropolis. He was also an evil man, but Lois hadn't been able to prove it yet. The only thing stopping Lex from controlling all of Metropolis was Superman, and Lex would never control the Man of Steel. Instead, Lex must have tried to make a super-clone.

Before Lois could finish reading, she heard shouts and footsteps coming from a nearby stairwell. She looked over at Bizarro, but he didn't seem worried.

He may not realize Dr. Teng will be angry, Lois thought. *There's so much he doesn't understand.*

"Can you carry me and this computer away from here?" Lois asked the creature.

Bizarro smiled. "Me can do that," he said. Bizzaro lifted the heavy computer with one arm and grabbed Lois with the other.

Suddenly, the lab door flew open. Several guards rushed into the room. They all held strange glowing rods in their hands.

A man in a lab coat behind them spoke up. "Stop that monster!" he shouted. "Don't let Bizarro escape with that computer!"

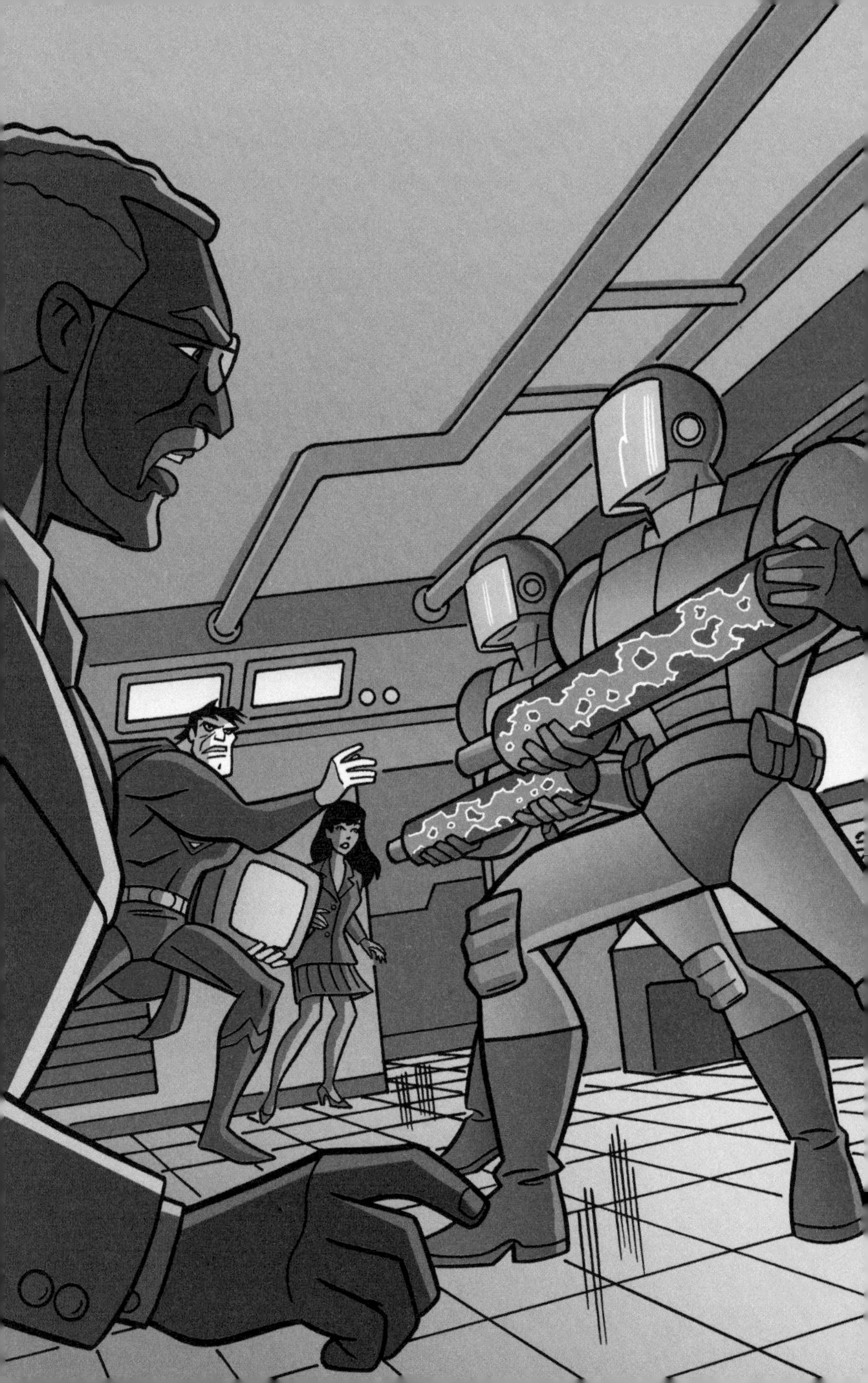

"Dr. Teng, why you yell?" asked Bizarro. "This am Lois Lane. She are my friend."

The guards pointed the glowing rods at Bizarro and Lois. Bright lights flashed outward from their tips. *BZZT!* Bizarro stepped in front of Lois to protect her.

FZZT! Electric beams struck Bizarro's back. Then one beam hit the computer. It shattered into a hundred pieces.

"Me save you again, Lois," Bizarro said. He swept her up in his arms and flew out of the hole in the wall.

"He's gone!" Dr. Teng said. "Clear the building! I need to destroy the evidence."

Bizarro hovered above the lab and frowned. "Why Dr. Teng call me Bizarro monster?" he said. "Me am not monster. Me am not Bizarro. Me am Superman!"

CHAPTER 4

SUPERMAN TO THE RESCUE

Superman hovered in the air, scanning the mountains with his super-vision. He didn't see Lois or the impostor anywhere.

Suddenly, he spotted the creature flying away with Lois in his arms. They seemed to come out of nowhere. Then Superman realized what had happened.

Bizarro had carried Lois from a hole in the building behind him. Superman hadn't seen them before because he couldn't see into the building. That meant the walls were lined with lead.

Somebody doesn't want me to know what is happening in there, Superman thought. He wanted to investigate, but first he had to save Lois.

Before he could reach her, there was a flash and an explosion. **BOOM!** The secret building blew into a million pieces. Smoke billowed into the air. Chunks of concrete flew everywhere.

Bizarro held Lois carefully, protecting her as rocks fell all around them. "That was my home," he cried. "Now it all gone!"

"I'm sorry," Lois said.

"Me take you away from here," the clone said.

Superman was confused. He could see that Lois's kidnapper looked like a monster, but Lois didn't seem to be frightened.

Superman quickly flew toward them. "Superman!" Lois cried.

"That not Superman! *Me* am!" Bizarro said. "That man am fake! He are wearing my Superman suit!"

"Put Lois down, impostor!" Superman shouted. "This is between you and me."

"Me not impostor!" Bizarro screamed. He flew to the mountainside, and set Lois on a cliff. "You safe here," Bizarro said.

Then, he turned toward Superman and shouted, "Me am SUPERMAN!"

Bizarro's eyes began to glow. Then two ice-blue beams zoomed toward Superman.

ZZRRRRTT! ZZRRRRTT!

The ice-beams zapped Superman right on the "S" on his chest.

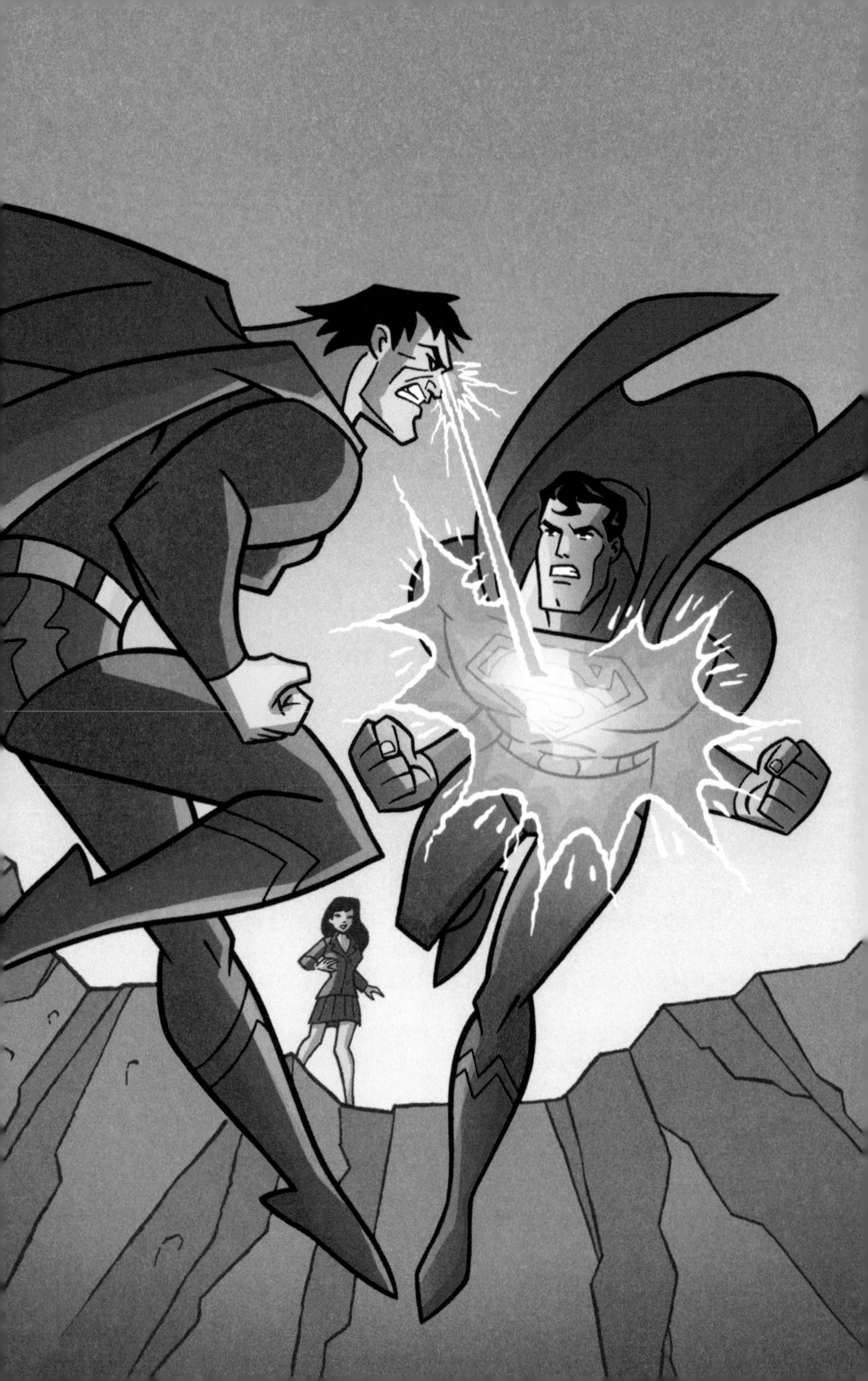

Superman was surrounded by a thick, super-cold wall of ice. He plummeted toward the earth like a giant blue rock.

"Yay! Me stop fake Superman!" Bizarro said. "Now me help people!"

Bizarro snatched up Lois and flew down to the city toward a construction project. A giant wrecking ball was about to slam into an abandoned building.

"Men going to break building!" Bizarro said. "Me stop ball and save building from men!"

"Stop!" Lois shouted. "They're just doing their jobs!"

It was too late. Bizarro flew toward the old building. As he floated past the construction site, he held up his hand to stop the wrecking ball.

Meanwhile, Superman hit the ground. The ice that surrounded him shattered. Then he flew toward Lois. Before the ball hit Bizarro, Superman plucked Lois from his arms.

CRASH!! The wrecking ball smashed into Bizarro, slamming him into the old building.

"It's Superman!" a construction worker yelled. "And he's fighting . . . Superman?!"

The wall began to crumble. The whole building collapsed on top of Bizarro, burying him in bricks and dust.

Lois was worried. "Bizarro isn't hurt, is he?" she asked.

"His name is Bizarro?" Superman asked. He saw with his X-ray vision that Bizarro was digging his way out of the bricks.

"He's fine," Superman said. "He's invulnerable, like I am. He seems to have all of my powers too — a bizarre version of them, anyway."

"Bizarro may look like a monster, but he's not evil," Lois said. She explained that Dr. Teng had helped Lex Luthor make a Superman clone.

Suddenly, Bizarro burst from the bricks. "Lois! Where is you?" he yelled.

Then he saw Lois in Superman's arms. "No!" he shouted at Superman. "Put Lois down, you fake! Me save you again, Lois!"

Bizarro zoomed toward them, but Superman zipped out of Bizarro's way. Bizarro flew right past them.

"This isn't Bizarro's fault," Lois told Superman. "He didn't ask to be made."

"He's just trying to be helpful," Lois continued. "He thinks like a very small child. Please don't hurt him, Superman."

Superman could see that Lois was right. He didn't want to hurt Bizarro, but he couldn't let Bizarro hurt anyone else.

"He's too reckless. I have to stop him," he said. "But don't worry, Lois. I'll find a way to do it without hurting him."

Lois's face lit up. "I have an idea!" she said. "You have to let Bizarro defeat you."

"What do you mean?" Superman asked.

Lois whispered in Superman's ear.

"That's a great plan!" Superman said. "And I know just how we can do it."

CHAPTER 5

BIZARRO SUPERMAN

Superman soared away with Lois in his arms. "We need to lead Bizarro toward Project Cadmus," he whispered.

Lois looked back. "Slow down a little," she said. "We want him to catch up."

Bizarro flew after them. "Lois not worry!" he shouted. "Me coming!"

Superman came to a stop above a steep hillside. "Cadmus is right below us. Are you ready, Lois?" he asked.

"I'm ready," Lois said.

Bizarro flew right to them. "Me save you from fake Superman!" he shouted. He scooped Lois gently from Superman's arms.

"Thank you, Superman," Lois said to Bizarro.

Bizarro smiled. "Lois remember who me am now!" he exclaimed.

"I'm sorry your old home blew up," Lois said. "But under that mountain is a new secret lab where you can live!"

"A secret lab?" he asked.

"This lab even has a secret jail where you can lock up the bad guys," she replied.

Bizarro frowned. "Lois, if it secret, how you know where it is?"

"Because —" Lois stuttered. Maybe Bizarro wasn't so dumb after all.

Superman realized he had to get Bizarro's attention. "Hey, Bizarro," he yelled. "Give Lois back to me!"

"No!" Bizarro said. He zoomed toward Superman. He grabbed the Man of Steel by the end of his red cape, and he said, "Me put you in jail!" Then Bizarro threw him, with all his might, toward the earth.

As Superman fell, he saw that he was headed in the right direction.

BOOM! He crashed hard into the mountain and broke through the roof of the Cadmus lab. Finally, he landed in a large room filled with science equipment.

WHAM! The scientists stopped their work and stared at Superman. The chief scientist, Dr. Emil Hamilton, stepped forward.

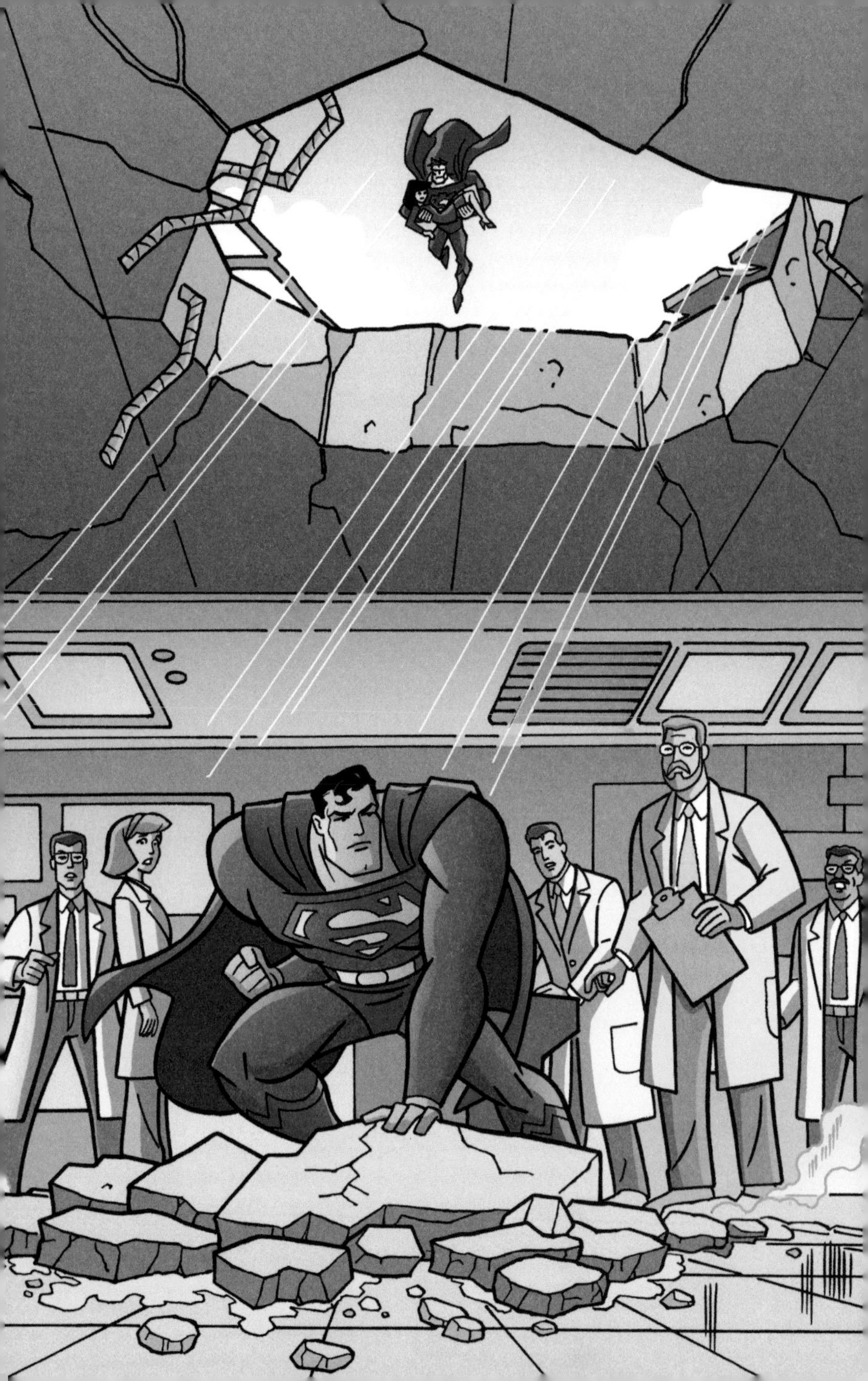

"Superman!" he said. "What are you doing here? What's going on?"

Superman looked through the hole in the ceiling. Bizarro was flying toward him with Lois in his arms.

Quickly, Superman told Dr. Hamilton about Bizarro. He explained what he wanted the scientists to do.

When Superman had finished explaining the plan, the scientists nodded in agreement. "We'll help you, Superman," Dr. Hamilton said.

Bizarro flew into the lab. SLAM! He landed right beside Superman.

Superman pretended to look sad. "You beat me!" he said slowly. "I give up."

"You under arrest, Super-fake!" Bizarro said. "Men, put him in secret jail."

The scientists led the real Superman out of the lab, but Dr. Hamilton stayed behind.

"You had a busy day," Lois said to Bizarro. "You stopped those cars. You saved me three times. Your home blew up, and a building fell on you. You chased the fake-Superman all over Metropolis. And now you have a new home. You must be very tired after all that."

Bizarro put Lois down on the floor. "Me *am* tired," he said.

"That's okay," Lois said. "Your new, secret bed is right here." She pointed to a large metal box in the center of the room. "It's a lot like your old bed, isn't it?"

Bizarro smiled. "I like that!" he said.

Dr. Hamilton pressed a button. **CLICK!** The glass cover slid over the metal bed.

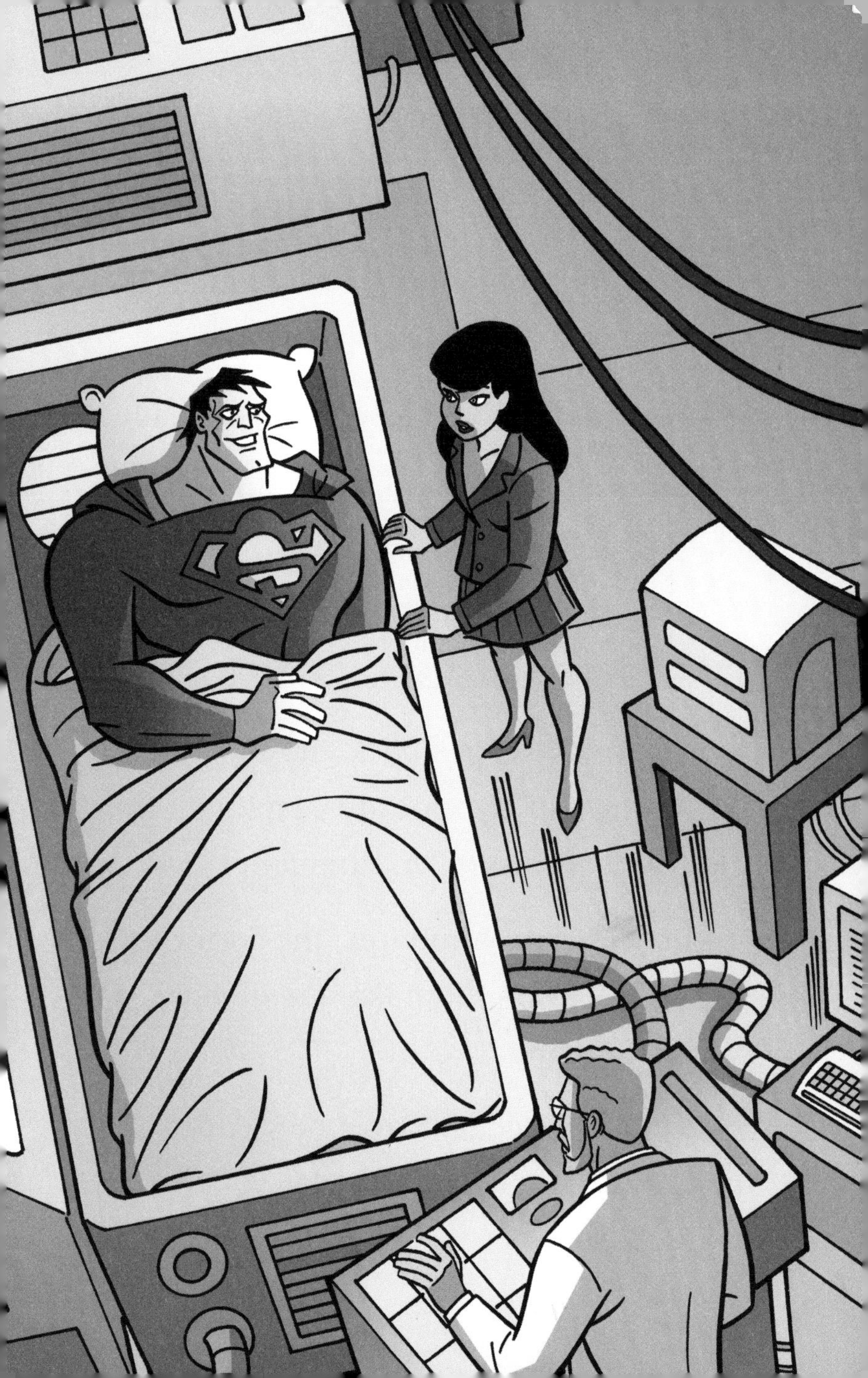

Bizarro yawned. He laid on his back in the metal bed and closed his eyes.

Dr. Hamilton handed Lois a blanket. She gently tucked Bizarro in.

"Good night, friend Lois," Bizarro said.

Lois smiled at Bizarro. "You did a good job today. Sleep tight, Superman," she said.

In less than a minute, Bizarro was asleep. The glass cover slid shut.

Superman stepped back into the room. "How long will Bizarro stay sleeping in that chamber?" he asked Dr. Hamilton.

"Until we wake him up," the doctor said. "While he sleeps, I'll make sure he has pleasant dreams."

Superman nodded. Then he scooped Lois up and carried her into the sky.

Lois sighed. "I feel bad that we had to trick Bizarro," she said. "He tried so hard to be a good super hero."

"He's just too dangerous," Superman said. "It had to be done."

"I can't wait to write this story," Lois said. "I just wish I could prove that Lex Luthor was responsible for cloning you."

"Just don't say where we hid Bizarro," Superman said. "Lex will try to find him."

Moments later, Superman set Lois down on the roof of the Daily Planet Building. They watched the sun as it set over the Metropolis skyline.

"In some ways, Bizarro really was like you," Lois said. "He tried to use his powers to help Metropolis. He just didn't quite understand how to do it."

"In his dreams, Bizarro won't make mistakes," Superman said. "He can be the super hero he wants to be — he can be *me*."

Lois looked out at the Metropolis skyline and smiled.

"Well," she said, "I don't think anyone could ever take your place, Superman."

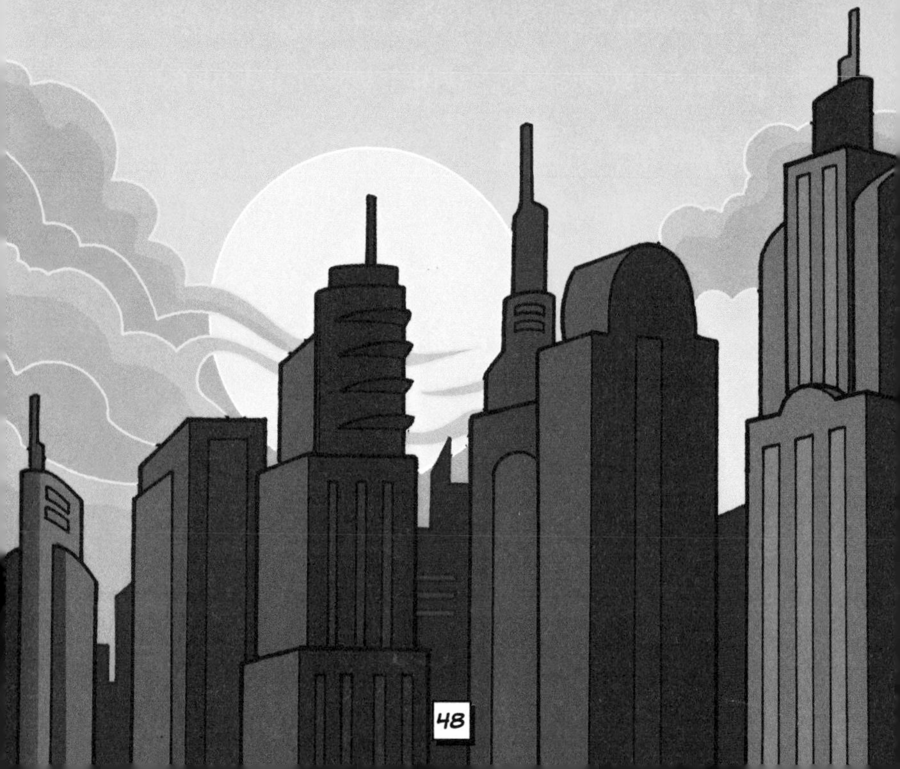

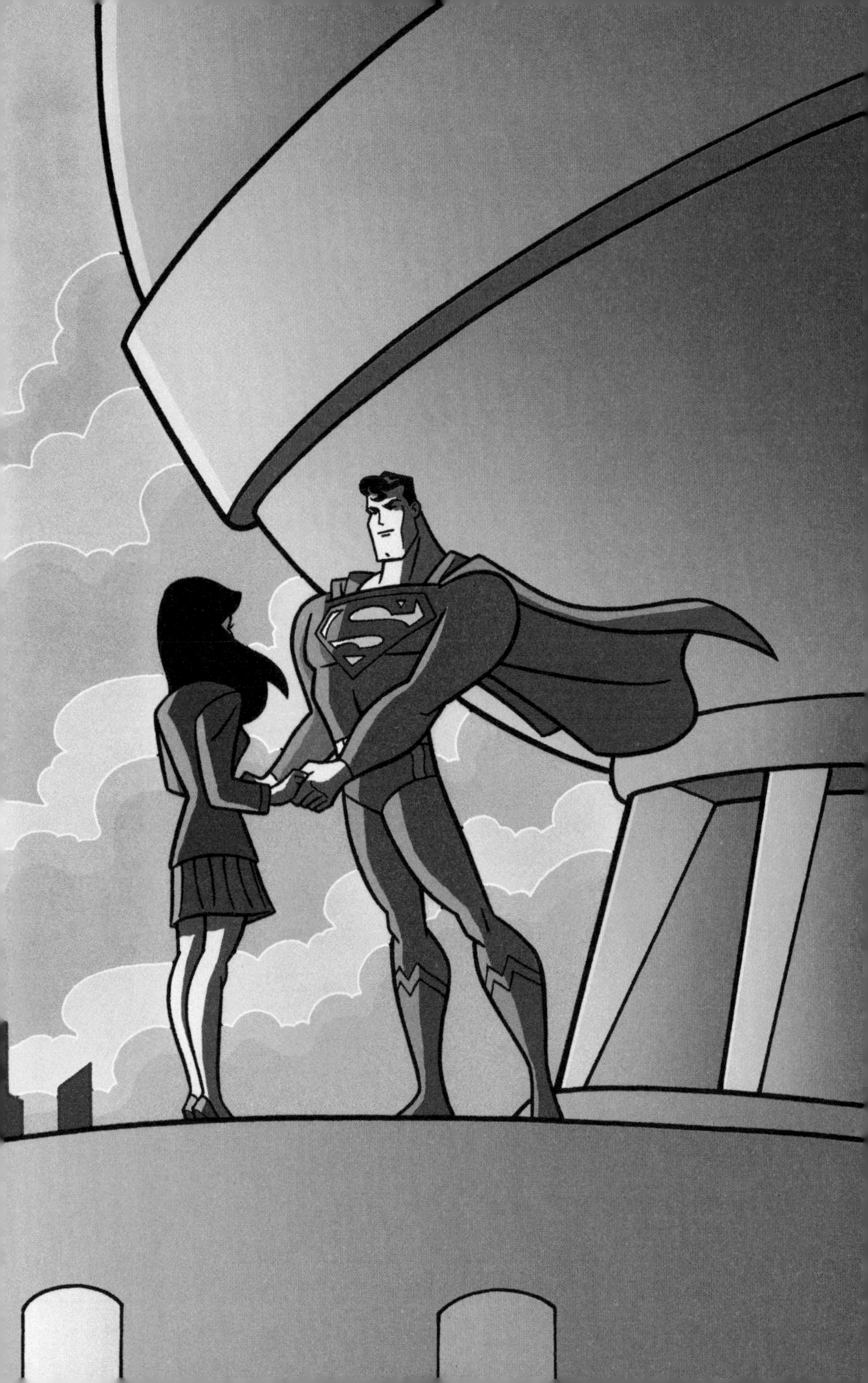

DAILY PLANET

FROM THE DESK OF CLARK KENT

WHO IS BIZARRO?

Bizarro is similar to a small child in many ways. He is wide-eyed and innocent, having been recently brought into existence. He does not grasp *right* and *wrong*, and his good intentions often end up causing more problems. He is extremely emotional, and he does not consider the negative outcomes of his actions. But Bizarro is different from a little child in one big way — he has the strength and speed of the Man of Steel himself. Bizarro is unpredictable and doesn't know his own power, which makes him a real menace to Metropolis.

- Bizarro's superpowers are completely opposite from the Man of Steel. Instead of Superman's fiery heat vision, Bizarro blasts beams of ice from his eyes. And, while Superman can breathe gusts of cold air, Bizarro burps deadly flames.

- Superman's greatest weaknesses also have the opposite affect on Bizarro. While kryptonite can bring the Man of Steel to his knees, the radioactive rock makes Bizarro even stronger.

- Even mutated clones need a friendly pet. Bizarro stole his pet from the Interplanetary Zoo in Superman's Fortress of Solitude. Like his master, Bizarro's pet, Krypto, is the opposite of normal. To show excitement and love, Krypto doesn't wag its tail — it bites!

- Like the real Man of Steel, Bizarro feels a strong bond with Daily Planet reporter Lois Lane and wants to protect her. Because Superman can already handle that job, Bizarro created a clone of Miss Lane. Bizarro Lois Lane is exactly like the real version of the reporter — except for her mutated, zombie-like appearance!

BIOGRAPHIES

Louise Simonson writes about monsters, science fiction and fantasy characters, and superheroes. She wrote the award-winning *Power Pack* series, several best-selling X-Men titles, *Web of Spider-man* for Marvel Comics, and *Superman: Man of Steel* and *Steel* for DC Comics. She has also written many books for kids. She is married to comic artist and writer Walter Simonson and lives in the suburbs of New York City.

Erik Doescher is a freelance illustrator based in Dallas, Texas. Erik illustrated for a number of comic studios throughout the 1990s, and then moved to Texas to pursue videogame development and design. However, he still illustrates his favorite comic book characters.

Mike DeCarlo is a longtime contributor of comic art whose range extends from Batman and Iron Man to Bugs Bunny and Scooby-Doo. He resides in Connecticut with his wife and four children.

Lee Loughridge has been working in comics for more than 14 years. He currently lives in sunny California in a tent on the beach.

GLOSSARY

clone (KLOHN)—to make a copy of something

collapsed (kuh-LAPSD)—fell down suddenly from weakness

evidence (EV-uh-duhnss)—information or items that help prove something

impostor (im-POSS-tur)—someone who pretends to be someone he or she is not

investigate (in-VESS-tuh-gate)—to find out as much as possible about something

invulnerable (in-VUHL-nur-uh-buhl)—impossible to be harmed or damaged

reckless (REK-liss)—careless and without regard to the safety of other people

shattered (SHAT-urd)—broke into tiny pieces

smother (SMUTH-ur)—to cover completely

surveyed (sur-VAYD)—looked at the whole of a scene

DISCUSSION QUESTIONS

1. Bizarro was trying to help people, but he ended up causing a lot of trouble. Is Bizarro responsible for the damage he caused? Why or why not?

2. Some people think cloning humans should be illegal. What do you think?

3. Superman can fire lasers from his eyes and breathe super-cold air. Bizarro can belch fire and shoot ice-beams from his eyes. Who has better superpowers — Superman or Bizarro? Why?

WRITING PROMPTS

1. Bizarro doesn't quite understand the harm that he causes. Rewrite your favorite part of this story from Bizarro's perspective.

2. Bizarro pretends to be Superman. Imagine that someone is pretending to be just like you. Make a list of things you could do to prove that your impostor is a fake.

3. Imagine that Bizarro escapes and once again puts Metropolis in danger. Write about how Superman stops Bizarro.

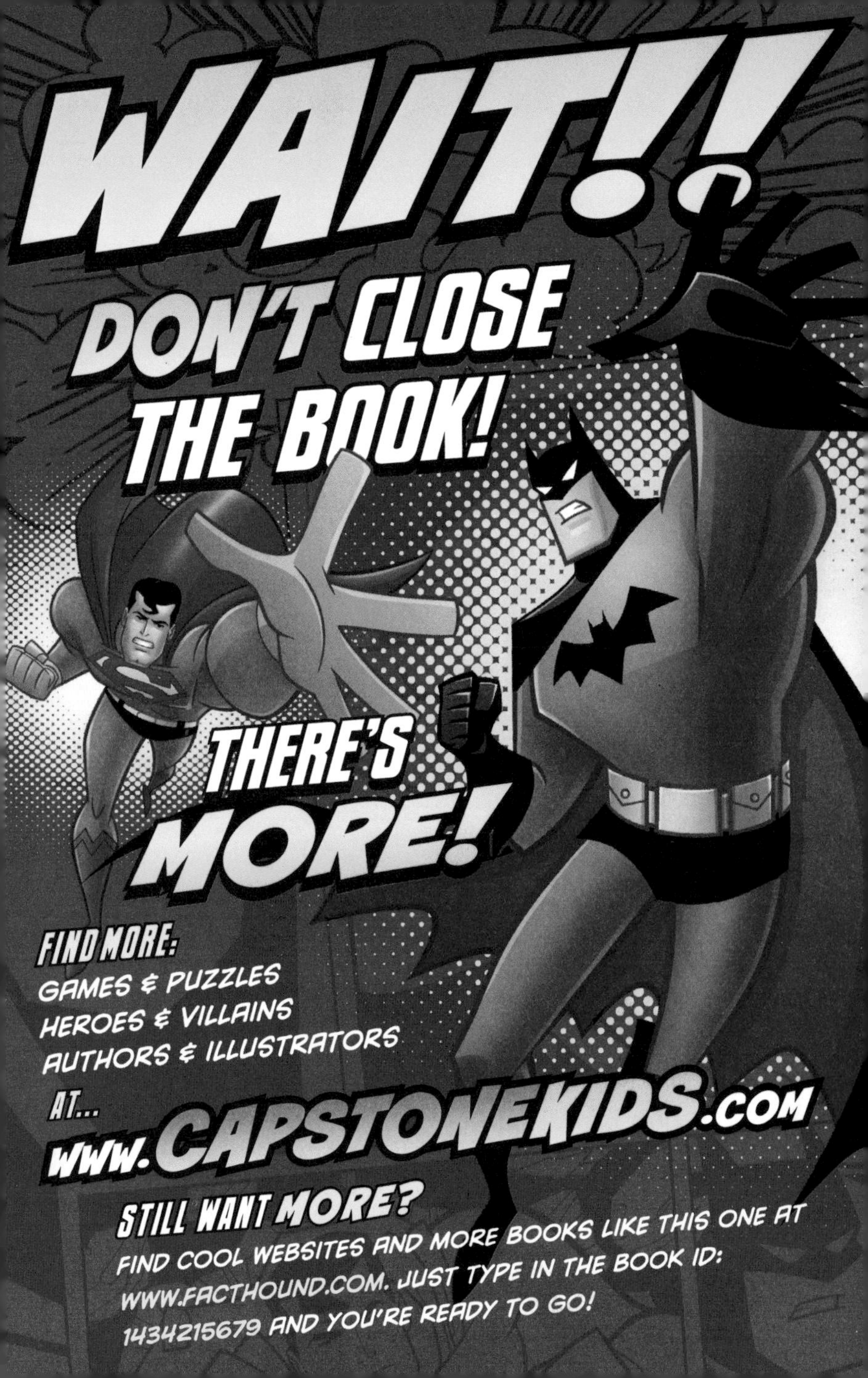
WAIT!!
DON'T CLOSE THE BOOK!
THERE'S MORE!
FIND MORE:
GAMES & PUZZLES
HEROES & VILLAINS
AUTHORS & ILLUSTRATORS
AT...
www.CAPSTONEKIDS.com
STILL WANT MORE?
FIND COOL WEBSITES AND MORE BOOKS LIKE THIS ONE AT
WWW.FACTHOUND.COM. JUST TYPE IN THE BOOK ID:
1434215679 AND YOU'RE READY TO GO!

MORE NEW SUPERMAN ADVENTURES!

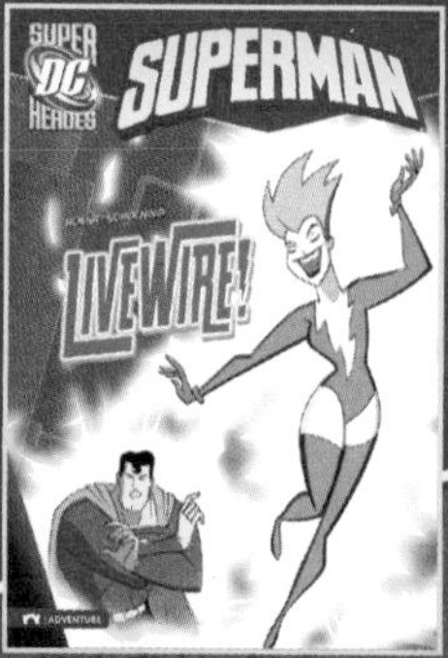
SUPER DC HEROES
SUPERMAN
LIVEWIRE!

LIVEWIRE!

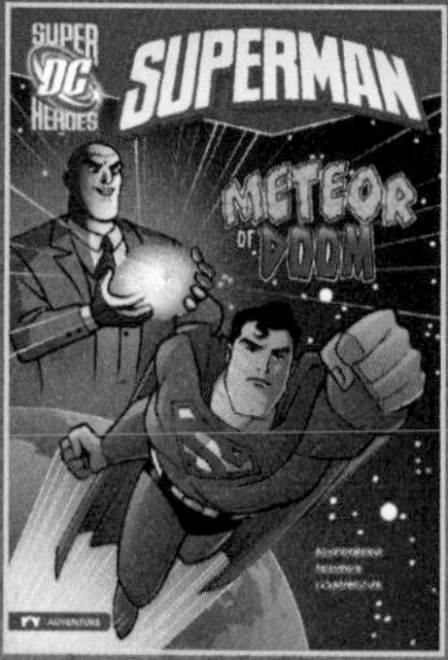
SUPER DC HEROES
SUPERMAN
METEOR OF DOOM

METEOR OF DOOM

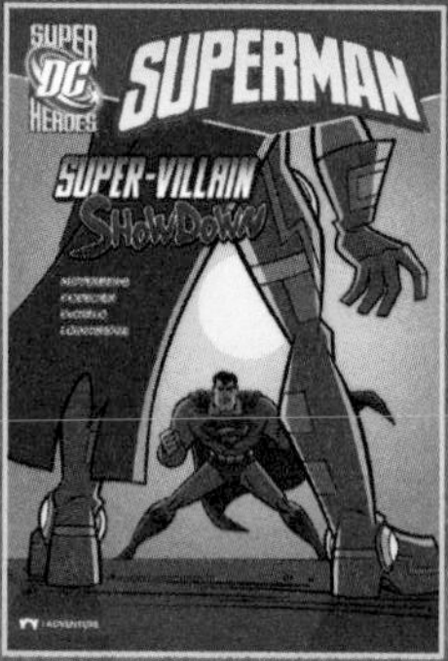
SUPER DC HEROES
SUPERMAN
SUPER-VILLAIN SHOWDOWN

SUPER-VILLAIN SHOWDOWN

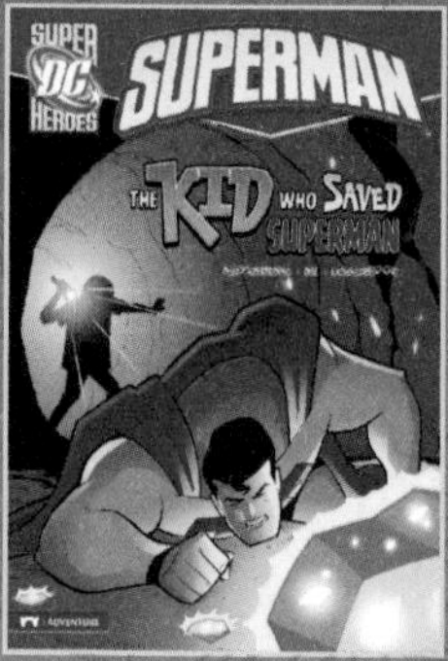
SUPER DC HEROES
SUPERMAN
THE KID WHO SAVED SUPERMAN

THE KID WHO SAVED SUPERMAN

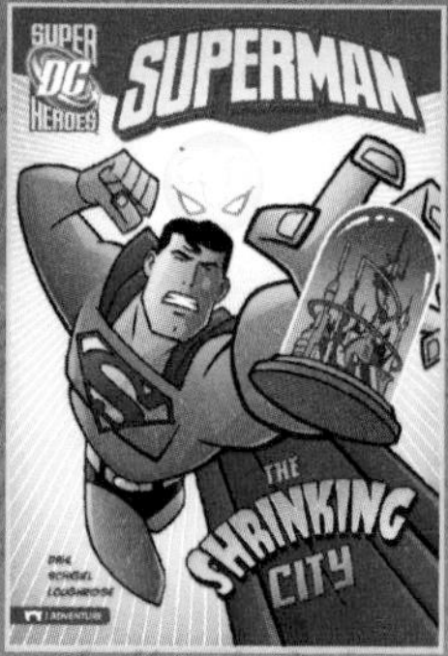
SUPER DC HEROES
SUPERMAN
THE SHRINKING CITY

THE SHRINKING CITY

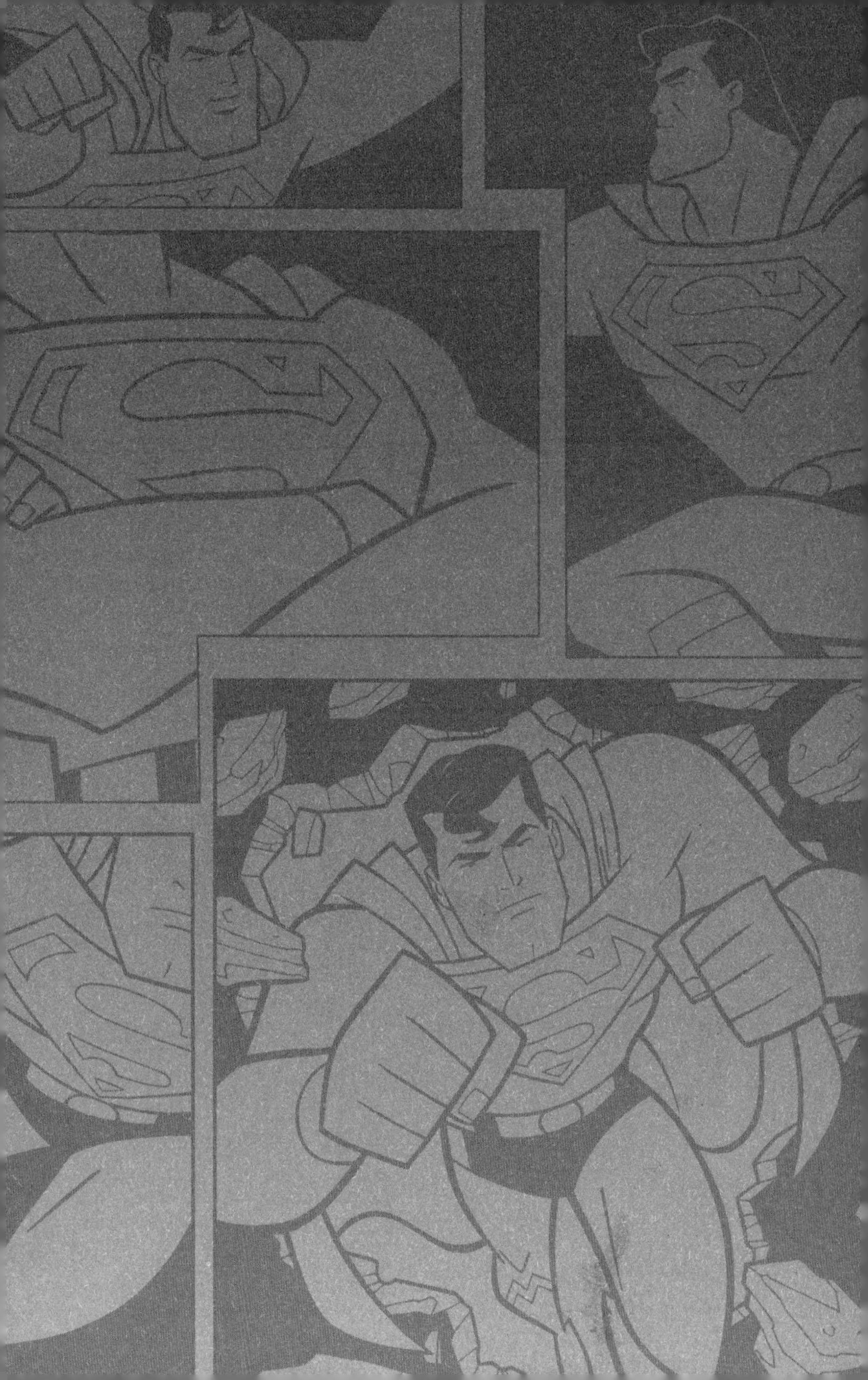

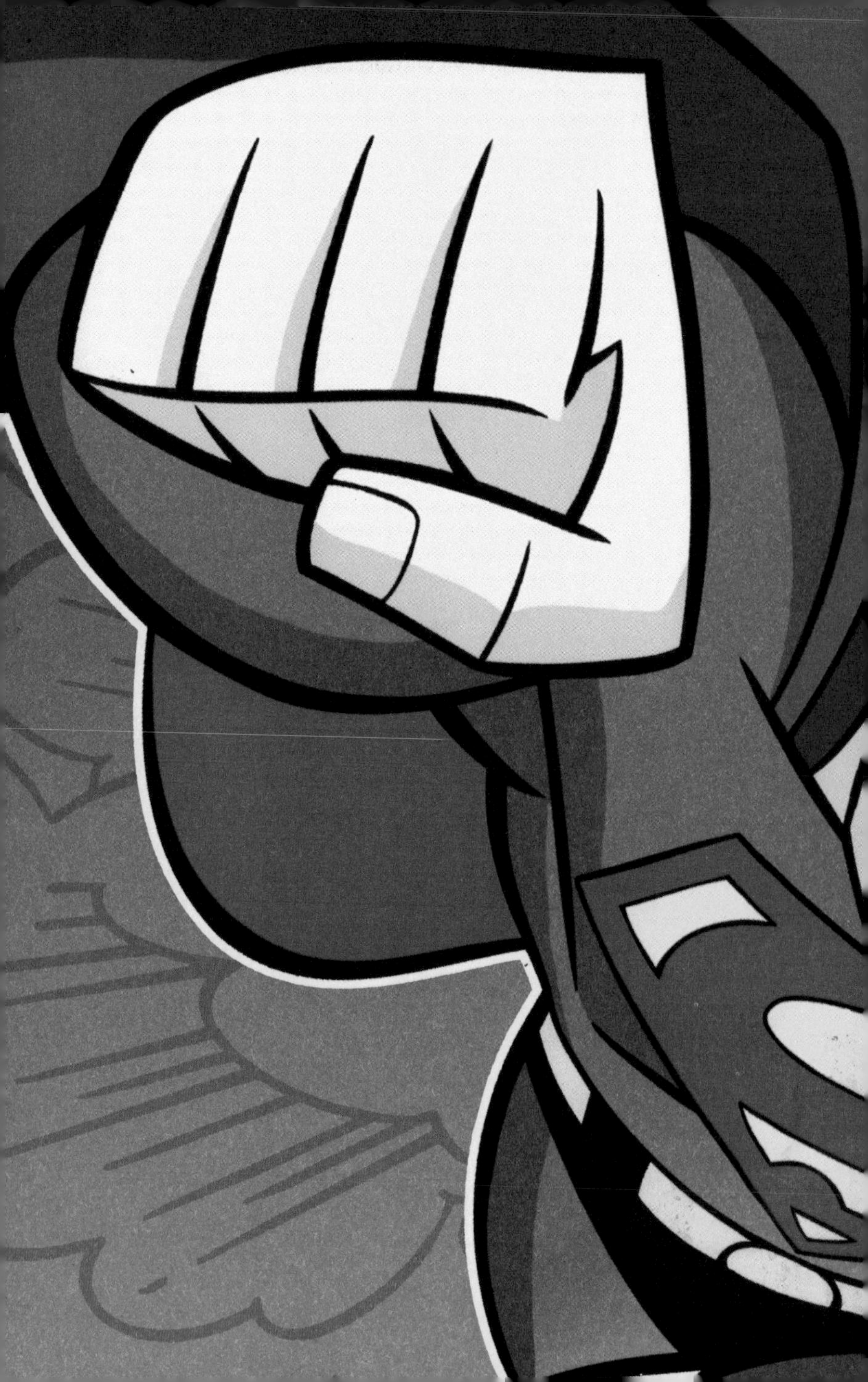